For Shauna, Heather, Danielle, Matthew, Tyler, Caelan,
Isabelle, and Matisse, the grandchildren in my life.

And for children the world over who help grown-ups shed
their seriousness and remember to imagine, laugh and play.

This book was a gift to _____

From_____ Date _____

REMEMBERING WHEN I WAS YOUNG

A Fun, Imaginative World You Create with Your Child or Grandchild

Story by Carole Carson with Illustrations by Peggy Kenfield

Published by
Hound Press
PO Box 2328
Nevada City, CA 95959

Kathi Dunn, Designer
Carolyn Crane, Editor
Joni Mahler, Editor

Printed in China

ISBN-13: 978-0-9766030-8-5
ISBN-10: 0-9766030-8-X

Remembering
WHEN I WAS YOUNG

Carole Carson

Peggy Kenfield

Limited First Edition

Hound Press

Nevada City, California

YOU ASKED ME, DEAR GRANDCHILD, WHAT IT WAS LIKE WHEN I WAS YOUNG? When I was

YOUR AGE?

kids PANTS were held up by GIANT BALLOONS

and CANARIES

were groomed

not POODLES

IN WINTER

the ICICLES came in 3 FLAVORs

while

SNOW FALL

was

BRIGHT

TURQUOISE
GREEN

HUGE dinosaurs EVERYWHERE!

TRUST MY THREE

EYES

We had just one number

FISH *swam in the* **SKY**

BIRDS *flew in the* **DEEP**

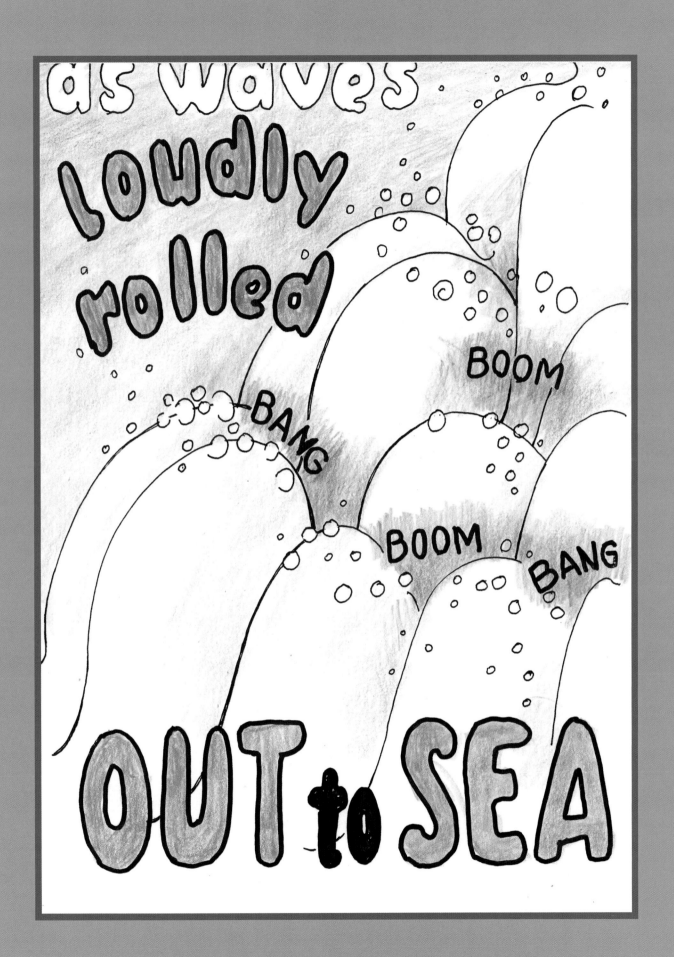

The SUN was BRIGHT

PURPLE

THE MOON

HOT

PINK

FLOWERS GREW UP COLORED BLACK

and
We always
had

PEBBLES

FOR

SNACKS

ELEPHANTS STOOD ONLY 2 inches HIGH

ZEBRAS had HUGE POLKA-DOTS

our WATER was ORANGE as it flowed up the SINK

and ICE CUBES were steaming, WHITE HOT

"Tomorrow" was Yesterday,

"NOW" never came,

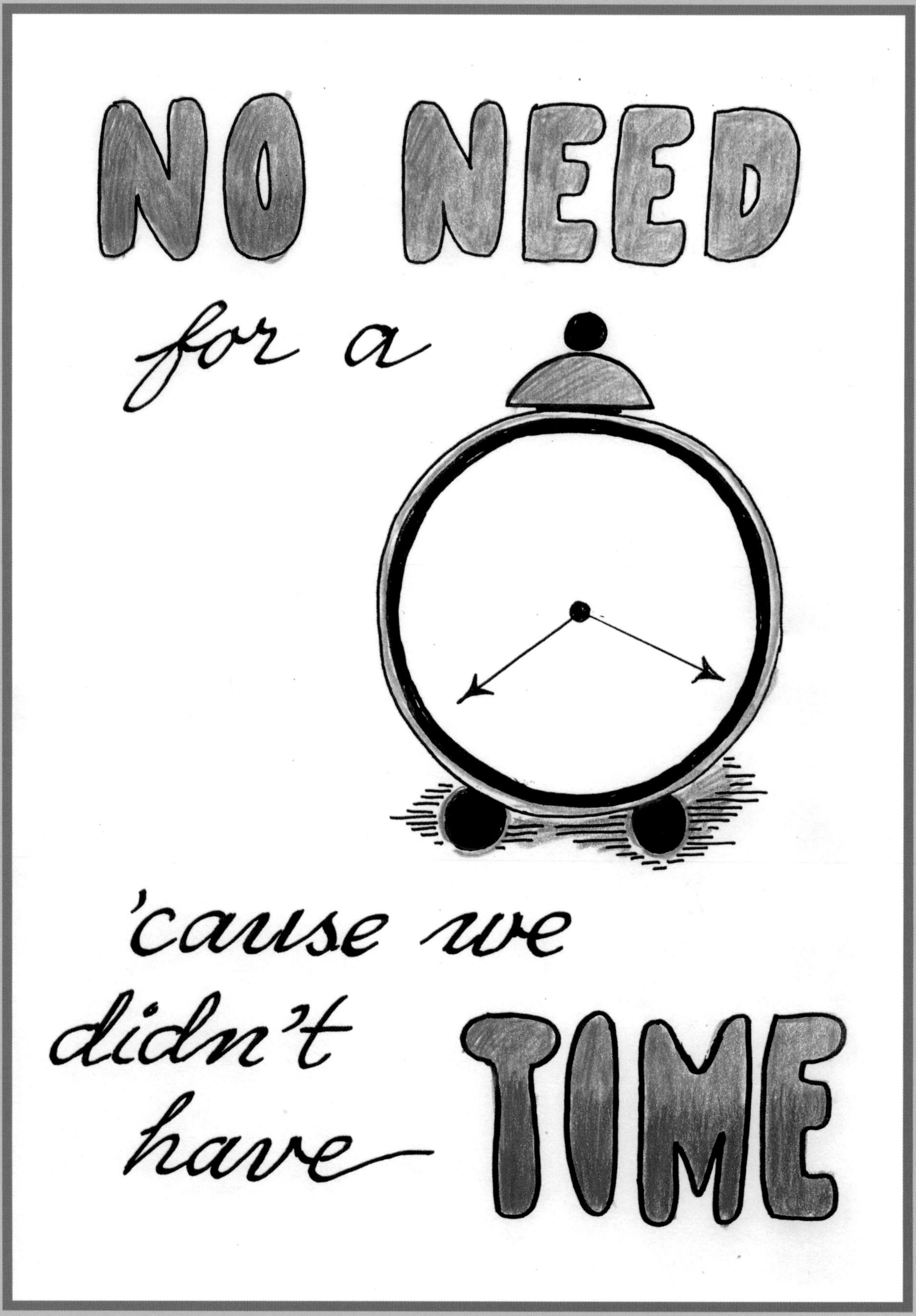
NO NEED
for a
'cause we
didn't
have
TIME

or **MONEY,**

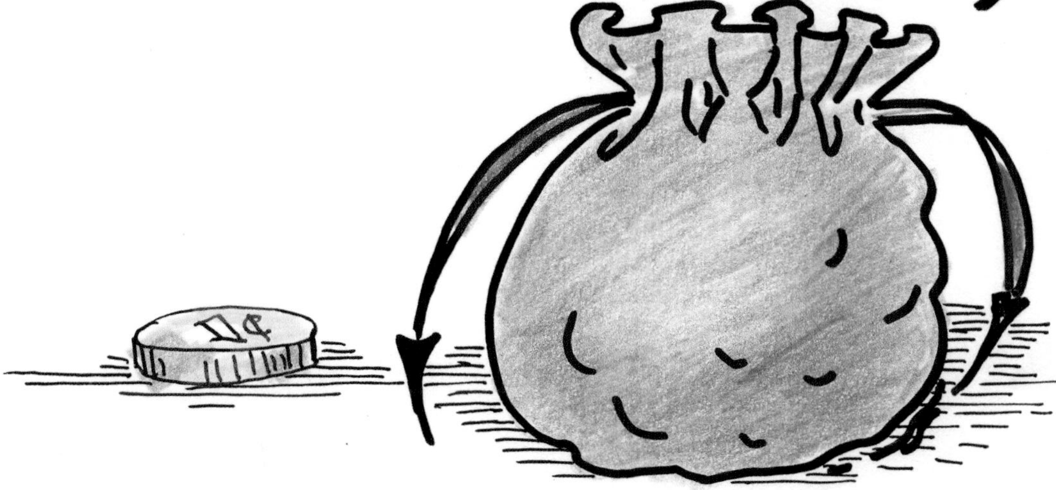

THINGS NEVER

were **SOLD**

It's FUN to Remember

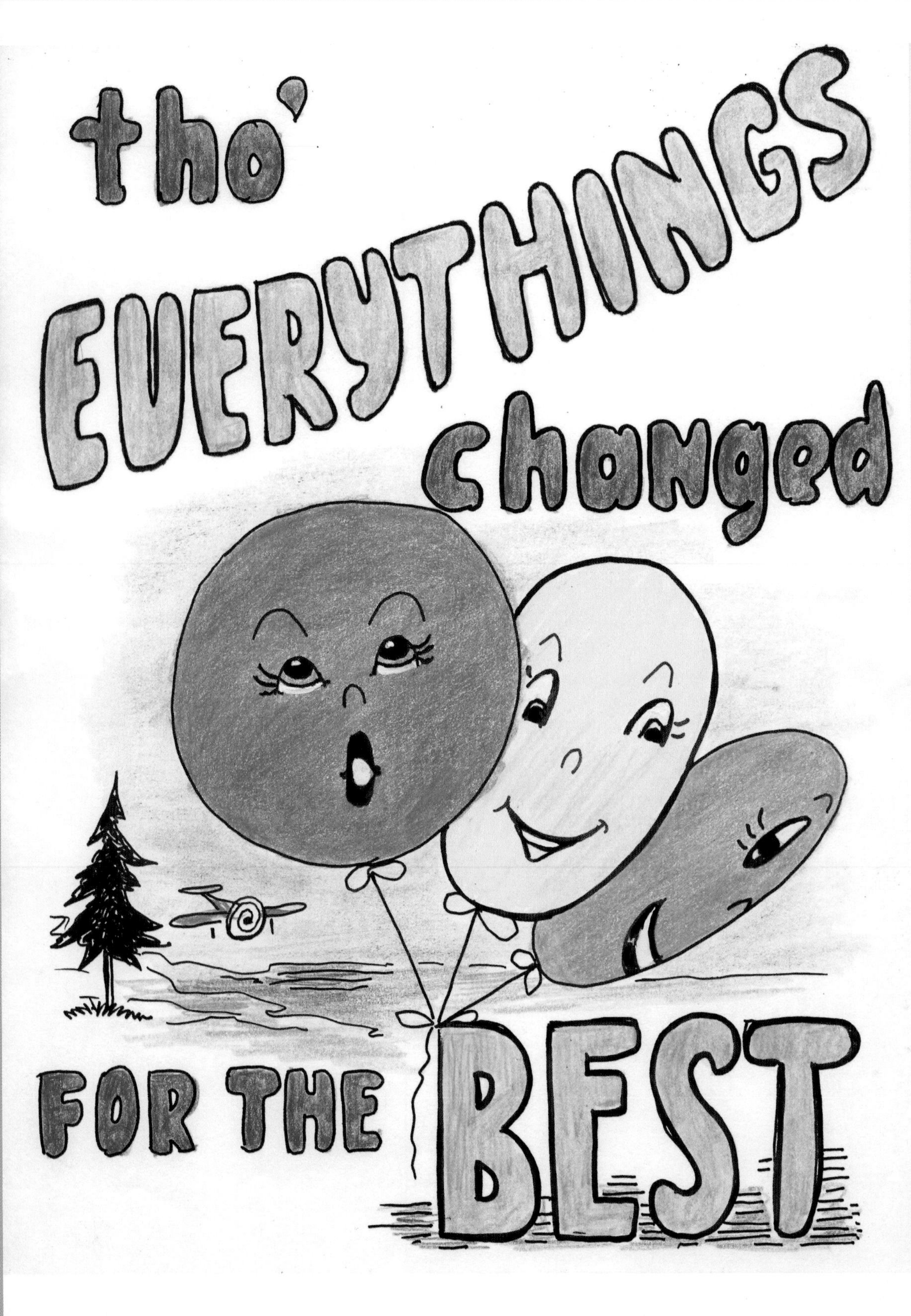
tho' EVERYTHINGS changed
FOR THE BEST

you'll have to

IMAGINE

???

HOW DIFFERENT IT WAS,

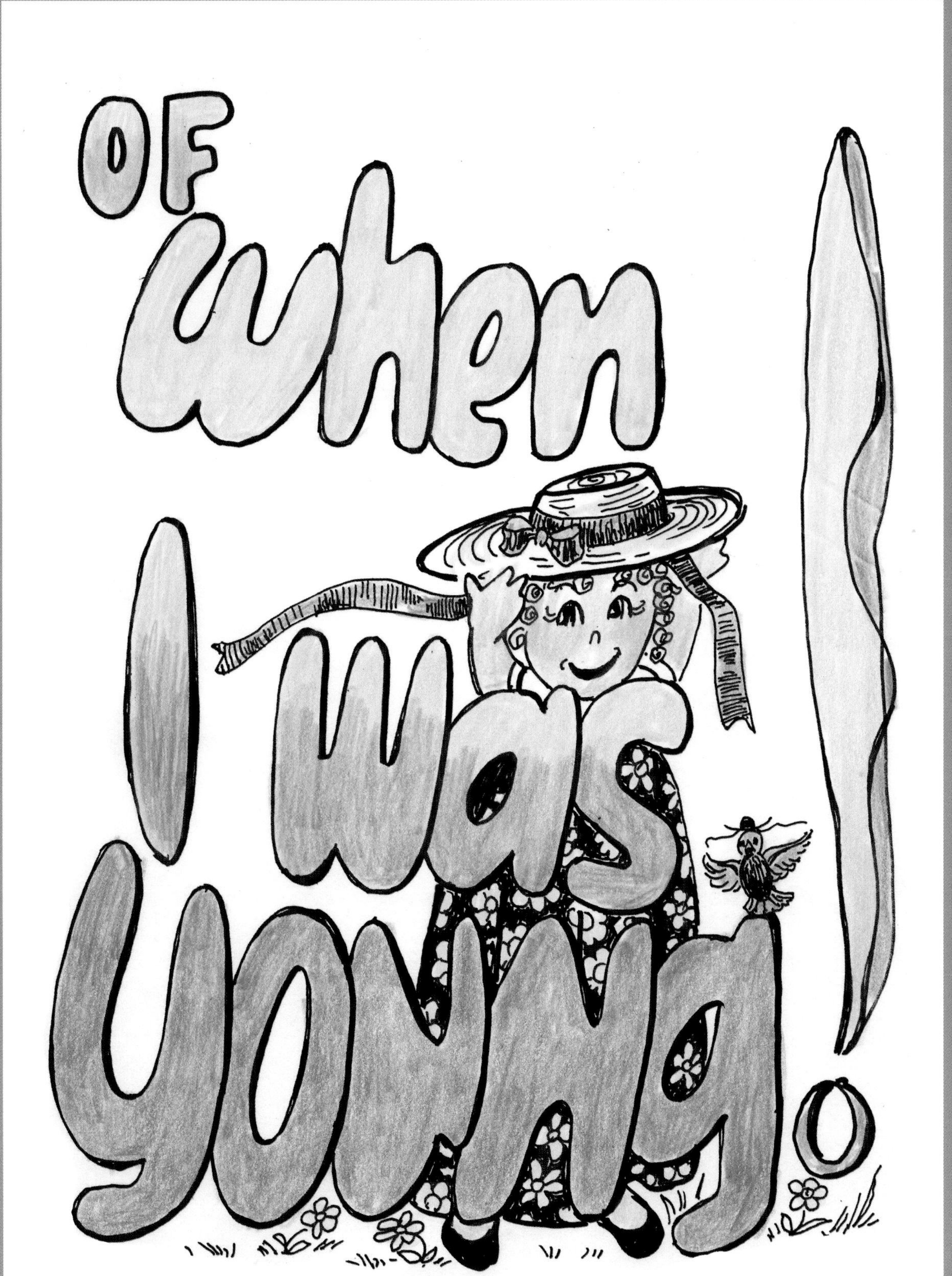
OF when I was young!

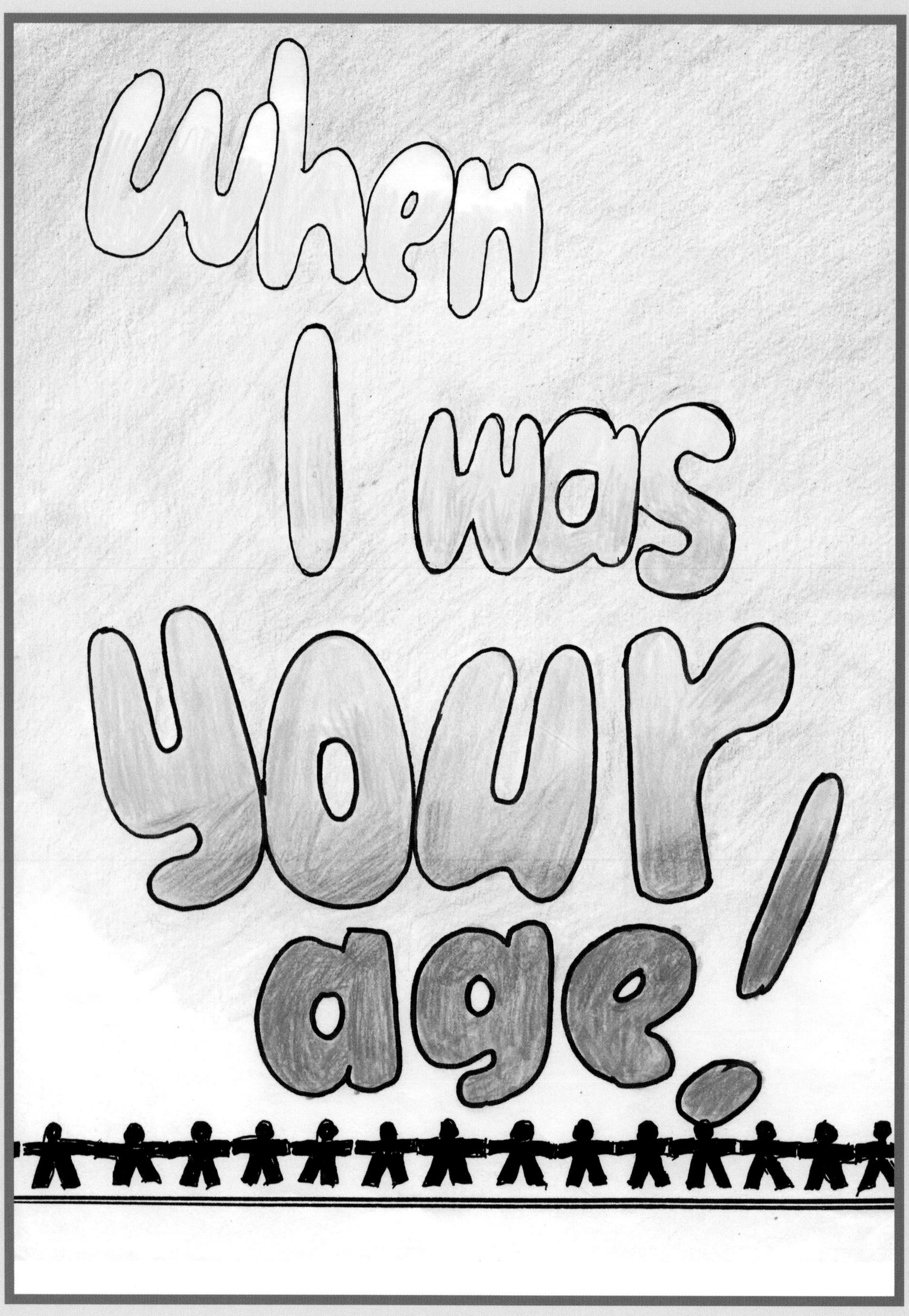
When I was your age!

FAMILY

Did you ever have a pet? What was your pet's name? _____
_____

What did it look like? _____
_____
_____

Did you have any brothers or sisters? What were their names?_____
_____
_____

Did you always get along?_____
_____

Did your parents make you do chores? _____
_____

Was your bedroom clean or messy? _____
_____

Where did you live? _____
_____

Was it hot or cold, or in between? _____
_____

Did you always live in the same house?_____
_____

Was it big or small, or in between? _____
_____

Did you get an allowance? How much? _____
What did you spend it on? _____
_____

Did your family eat all its meals together? What was your favorite meal?_____
_____
_____

Did you ever cook? What did you like to make?_____
_____
_____

FRIENDS

Did you have a make-believe friend? _____
_____
_____

Who was your best friend? _____
_____

Where did he or she live? _____
_____

What games did you play with your friends? _____
_____
_____

Did you ever get in trouble? _____
_____
_____
_____

GROWING UP

When did you have a boyfriend or girlfriend?_____
_____

Where did you go on dates? _____
_____
_____

When did you first drive a car? _____
_____

Whose car was it?_____
_____

When did you first have a car of your own? _____
_____

What color was it? _____
At what age did you feel grown up? _____
_____

PLAY

What kinds of toys did you have? _____
_____
_____

Did you ever make mud pies? _____
_____

Did you ever splash through puddles? _____
_____
_____

Did you watch television? _____
_____

What was your favorite show? _____
_____
_____

Did you listen to the radio? What was your favorite program? _____
_____
_____

Did you play sports? Which sports? _____
_____
_____

Did you make up plays or skits for your friends and family? _____
_____
_____

What was your favorite game? _____
_____
_____

What did you do over summer vacation? _____
_____

What was the best vacation you ever had? _____
_____
_____
_____
_____

MILESTONES

What was your favorite birthday?_____
_____
_____

What was your favorite birthday cake? _____
_____

What was the most exciting thing that happened in our nation when you were
a child? _____
_____
_____
_____

What was the biggest change you had to make? _____
_____
_____
_____

What did you want to be when you grew up?_____
_____
_____

Did you do it?_____
If you could change one thing, what would it be?_____
_____
_____
_____
_____
_____
_____
_____
_____
_____

Signed by _____ Date _____

Order Now!

Looking for a unique gift for grandparents? Or new parents? Maybe a special aunt who's having a birthday? Give a playful gift, one the family will cherish long after the toys have been put away. Be sure to order a set for yourself as well!

Remembering
When I Was Young

Story by
Carole Carson

Illustrations by
Peggy Kenfield

Matching
Coloring Book
Available!

**A Fun, Imaginative World
to Enjoy With Your
Child or Grandchild**

Remembering
When I Was Young

GIFT SET
Remembering
When I Was Young
(Standard Edition) and

Remembering
When I Was Young
(Coloring Book Edition)
$24.95

STANDARD EDITION
Remembering
When I Was Young
$19.95

COLORING BOOK
EDITION
Remembering
When I Was Young
$6.95

We have 4 convenient ways to order:

1. Order Online
Go to our website and place your order on our secure site.
Major credit cards accepted.

www.HoundPress.com

2. Order by Phone
Call with a credit card.

Toll free: 1 (800) 880-3172

3. Order by Secure Fax
Copy and fax the order form below. Order 24 hours, 7 days a week by credit card on our secure line.

FAX: 1 (530) 478-1108

4. Order by Mail
Copy and mail the order form below along with your check to:

Address:
Hound Press
PO Box 2328
Nevada City, CA 95959

ORDERING FORM

Product	Price		Quantity	Total
GIFT SET Remembering When I Was Young (Standard Edition) and Remembering When I Was Young (Coloring Book Edition)	$24.95	X		
STANDARD EDITION Remembering When I Was Young	$19.95	X		
COLORING BOOK EDITION Remembering When I Was Young	$6.95	X		
			Sub Total	
California Sales Tax: add 7.75% for purchases shipped to California addresses. Prices higher in Canada.				
Shipping: Allow ten days. USPS cost: $4.00 per order per gift set; $3.00 for book; $2.00 for coloring book.				
			Grand Total	

Hound Press

Send Order to:

Name: _____

Address: _____ Apt/Unit: _____

City: _____ State: _____ Zip: _____

Tel: _____ Email: _____